This book

belongs to

Claire Annette

Reading aloud with your child
opens the doors of true friendship.
This gentle routine will soon
become a pleasure for you both.
Your small effort of twenty minutes
every day for a few early years
will bear fruit for a lifetime.

B Read to Your UNNY

Rosemary Wells

SCHOLASTIC INC.
New York Toronto London Auckland Sydney
Mexico City New Dehli Hong Kong Buenos Aires

For information regarding permission, write to Permissions Department,

Scholastic Inc., 555 Broadway, New York, New York 10012.

ISBN-439-26091-4

12 11 10 9 8 7 6 5 4 3 2 1   1 2 3 4 5 6/0

First printing, September 1997

Printed in the U.S.A.

Read to your bunny often,

It's twenty minutes of fun.

It's twenty minutes of moonlight,

And twenty minutes of sun.

Twenty old-favorite minutes,

Twenty minutes brand-new,

Read to your bunny often,

And...

Your bunny will read to you.